This book belongs to

_____

_____

For Iris
C.F.

First published in 2009 in Great Britain by Gullane Children's Books
This edition published 2010 by

Gullane Children's Books
185 Fleet Street, London EC4A 2HS
www.gullanebooks.com

1   3   5   7   9   10   8   6   4   2

Text and illustrations © Charles Fuge 2009

The right of Charles Fuge to be identified as the author and illustrator of this work has been
asserted by him in accordance with the Copyright, Designs and Patents Act, 1988.

A CIP record for this title is available from the British Library.

ISBN: 978-1-86233-784-8

Printed and bound in China

WATCH OUT, Little Wombat!

written and illustrated by Charles Fuge

GULLANE
CHILDREN'S BOOKS

Little Wombat was playing explorers with Rabbit and Koala. "Let's go to the creek to hunt for the **Bunyip!**" he said.

"There's no such thing as a Bunyip, silly!"
laughed Rabbit and Koala.
"Oh yes there is! And I'm going
to find him," said Little Wombat.

And he marched off towards
the creek all by himself.

Little Wombat wandered up and down the creek, but there was no sign of a Bunyip. Then he had an idea — "I'll make my **own** Bunyip to fool Rabbit and Koala!" he giggled.

First Wombat piled up
the squishy mud and made
a monstery shape . . .

Then he gathered some old twigs for arms, black pebbles for eyes, pine cones for tusks and reeds for whiskers.

Koala and Rabbit were bored
of exploring without Wombat.
"Let's sneak up on him!" suggested Koala.
"And **roar** like a Bunyip!" laughed Rabbit.

The friends crept quietly down
to the creek and hid in the bushes.

"Now!" whispered Koala, and they jumped up with a booming "ROAR!" Little Wombat got such a fright that he fell, head-first, into his muddy monster.

Spinning round, Wombat was relieved
to see that it was only his friends.
But they weren't laughing . . . their
eyes were wide with terror!

"C-CROCODILE!"
they squealed, as they turned
and ran. Wombat spun
back round . . .

Towering above him was indeed an
ENORMOUS crocodile.

The crocodile took one
look at Wombat, who was covered
head-to-toe with mud and stones,
reeds and cones . . .

"BUNYIP!" it shrieked,
and with an enormous splash, disappeared
back into the creek. Little Wombat turned
and ran as fast as his legs would carry him.

Mrs Wombat was sitting quietly outside the burrow, when the three friends came rushing back. "Whatever is the matter...?" she asked as they clung tightly to her. "You look as though you've just seen a Bunyip!"

Little Wombat looked at his friends —
"There's no such thing as a Bunyip!"
he grinned, and they all fell about laughing.